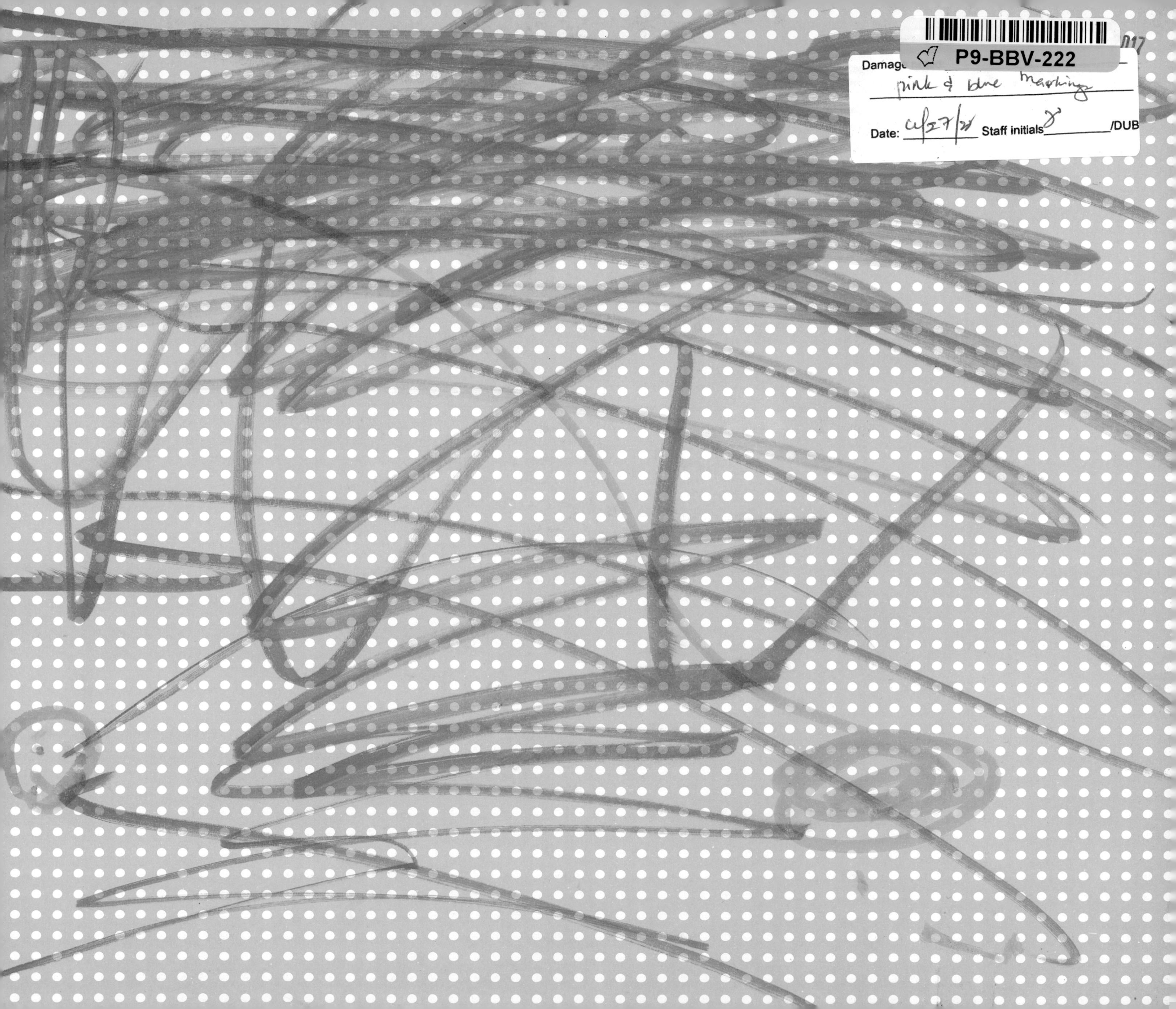

Peppa Pig

and the

Library Visit

This book is based on the TV series *Peppa Pig*.
Peppa Pig is created by Neville Astley and Mark Baker.

www.peppapig.com

First edition 2017

Library of Congress Catalog Card Number pending
ISBN 978-0-7636-9788-4

17 18 19 20 21 22 APS 10 9 8 7 6 5 4 3 2 1

Printed in Humen, Dongguan, China

This book was typeset in Peppa.
The illustrations were created digitally.

Candlewick Entertainment
an imprint of Candlewick Press
99 Dover Street
Somerville, Massachusetts 02144

visit us at www.candlewick.com

Peppa Pig and the Library Visit

CANDLEWICK
ENTERTAINMENT

It's bedtime for Peppa and George.

"Could we have a story, please?"

asks Peppa.

"Okay," says Mummy Pig.
"Here's the one about the red monkey."

"We always read that one," says Peppa.
"The red monkey takes a bath,

brushes his teeth,

and goes to sleep.
Let's choose another book instead."

Peppa goes to the bookshelf.

There's a book about a **blue tiger**,

a book about a
green spider,

a book about an
orange
penguin,
and . . .

"Ooh!" says Peppa.
"What's **this** one?"

"The Wonderful World of Concrete,"
reads Mummy Pig.

"I've been looking for that!"
says Daddy Pig.
"It's a book I borrowed
from the library."

12
1
2
3
4
5
6
7
8
9
10
11
1 2

"What's a library?" asks Peppa.

"A library is a place you can go to borrow books.
When you've finished reading them,
you take them back so others can borrow them,"
says Daddy Pig.

He looks at the book.

"I have had this for a rather long time," Daddy Pig says.

"You can return it tomorrow," says Mummy Pig,
"but right now, it's bedtime."

"After Daddy reads this story!"

Peppa insists.

Daddy Pig begins to read:

"The *Wonderful World* of Concrete.

Concrete is made of sand, water, and other things.

Chapter One: Sand!"

Sounds of snoring fill the room.
Peppa and George are fast asleep.

So is Mummy Pig!

The next morning,
Peppa and her family head to the library.

Peppa can't believe how many books are on the shelves.

"**Look at them all!**" she shouts.

"Shhh, Peppa," says Daddy Pig.

"You must be quiet in the library,

because people come here

to read and to be quiet."

"Next, please!"

comes another shout.

It's Miss Rabbit, the librarian.

"Hello, Mummy Pig," she says.

"Are you returning these books?"

"Yes, Miss Rabbit." Mummy Pig gives her books to Miss Rabbit to scan, and the computer beeps as the books slide across the counter.

"Why is the computer beeping?" asks Peppa.

"It's checking to see that you haven't been naughty and kept the book for too long."

"I may have kept this book for a bit too long," says Daddy Pig.

"Don't worry,"
says Miss Rabbit.

Then her computer
makes a loud, long beep.
"Daddy Pig!" she shouts.
"You've had this book out
for ten years!"

"Naughty Daddy!"

says Peppa.

Now that Daddy Pig's book is returned, he can borrow another one. Peppa and George want to borrow books, too.

Miss Rabbit shows Peppa and George to the children's section.

"Ooh!" says Peppa. "There are books about princesses, and animals, and planets!"

1 2 3

1 2

Danny Dog and Suzy Sheep
are at the library, too.
Danny Dog is borrowing
a book about soccer.
Suzy Sheep is borrowing
one about doctors.

George has chosen his book.
It's about dinosaurs!
"Dine-saw!" says George.
"Grrr!"

Daddy Pig has found an exciting new book:
Further Adventures in the World of Concrete.

"But Daddy Pig," says Peppa,

"I want a fun bedtime book!"

Mummy Pig pulls out a Red Monkey book.
"Not that again!" says Peppa. "It's boring."

"It's a different story," says Mummy Pig.
"Once upon a time, there was a red monkey— "

"I know," says Peppa.
"He had a bath,
brushed his teeth,
and went to sleep," she says.

"No," says Mummy Pig.
"He had **adventures**!"

"Ooh!" say the children.

They all gather around to see the book.

Peppa wants to hear the story.

"We can read it at home," says Mummy Pig.

"But I already chose a book about a princess," says Peppa.

Then she sees another book, about birds.

"That book looks interesting, too!"

Miss Rabbit has good news for Peppa:

"You can take up to three books home, if you'd like!"

"Yippee!" says Peppa.

"You just have to remember to bring them back on time," says Miss Rabbit. "And that goes for you, too, Daddy Pig."

Peppa laughs. "I'll make sure he remembers. I want to come back to the library all the time.

I love the library!"

Back at home, it's bedtime.

Mummy Pig opens the new Red Monkey book.

"Once upon a time, there was a red monkey.

He jumped in a space rocket and went to the moon."

"The moon!"

says Peppa.

"What an adventure!"

Mummy Pig turns the page.

"He had a picnic with a dinosaur."

"Dine-saw!" says George.

"Then the red monkey swam under the sea."

Mummy Pig turns the last page.

"Finally, he climbed the highest mountain.

That was a busy day!"

"I think Daddy Pig agrees," says Peppa.
Everyone looks. Daddy Pig is fast asleep.

"The end," whispers Mummy Pig. Sounds of Daddy Pig's snores fill the room. Everyone laughs.

What a fun day!